RAINBOW
magic

RUBY THE RED FAIRY
1-84362-016-2

AMBER THE ORANGE FAIRY
1-84362-017-0

SAFFRON THE YELLOW FAIRY
1-84362-018-9

FERN THE GREEN FAIRY
1-84362-019-7

SKY THE BLUE FAIRY
1-84362-020-0

IZZY THE INDIGO FAIRY
1-84362-021-9

HEATHER THE VIOLET FAIRY
1-84362-022-7

Collect all seven Rainbow Magic
books to bring the sparkle
back to Fairyland...

For everyone who has
felt fairy magic

Special thanks to
Sue Bentley

ORCHARD BOOKS
338 Euston Road, London NW1 3BH
Orchard Books Australia
Hachette Children's Books
Level 17/207 Kent Street, Sydney, NSW 2000
A Paperback Original
First published in Great Britain in 2003
Text © Working Partners Limited 2003
Created by Working Partners Limited, London W6 0QT
Illustrations © Georgie Ripper 2003
The right of Georgie Ripper to be identified as the illustrator
of this work has been asserted by her in accordance
with the Copyright, Designs and Patents Act, 1988.
A CIP catalogue record for this book is available
from the British Library.
ISBN 978 1 84362 022 8
27
Printed in Great Britain

Heather the Violet Fairy

by Daisy Meadows

illustrated by Georgie Ripper

ORCHARD BOOKS

Cold winds blow and thick ice form,
I conjure up this fairy storm.
To seven corners of the mortal world
the Rainbow Fairies will be hurled!

I curse every part of Fairyland,
with a frosty wave of my icy hand.
For now and always, from this fateful day,
Fairyland will be cold and grey!

All the Rainbow Fairies are together except
one! The fairies will never get their
Rainbow Magic back without
Heather the Violet Fairy

Contents

Message on
a Kite

"I can't believe this is the last day of our holiday!" said Rachel Walker. She gazed up at her kite as it rose in the clear blue sky.

Kirsty Tate watched the purple kite soar above the field beside Mermaid Cottage. "But we still have to find Heather!" she reminded Rachel.

Jack Frost's wicked spell had banished the seven Rainbow Fairies to Rainspell Island. And without the Rainbow Fairies, Fairyland had no colour! Kirsty and Rachel had already found Ruby, Amber, Saffron, Fern, Sky, and Izzy. Now there was just Heather the Violet Fairy left to find.

Rachel felt the kite tug on its string. She looked up. Something violet and silver flashed at the end of the kite's long tail. "Look up there!" she shouted. Kirsty shaded her eyes with her hand. "What is it? Do you think it's a fairy?" she asked. "I'm not sure," Rachel said, winding in the string.

As the kite came bobbing towards them, Kirsty saw that a long piece of violet-coloured ribbon was tied to its tail. She helped Rachel to untie the ribbon and smooth it out.

"It has tiny silver writing on it," Rachel said.

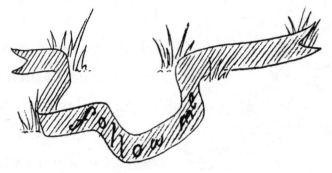

Kirsty crouched down to have a closer look. "It says, Follow me."

Suddenly the ribbon was lifted up by the breeze. It fluttered across the field.

"It must be leading us to Heather!" Kirsty said, jumping up.

Rachel rolled up her kite. "Mum, is it OK if we go exploring one last time?" she called.

Mrs Walker was talking to Kirsty's mum in the garden outside Mermaid Cottage. Kirsty's family was staying in Dolphin Cottage, next door. "Of course, as long as Kirsty's mum agrees," Mrs Walker replied.

"It's fine by me," said Mrs Tate.

"But don't go far. The ferry leaves at four o'clock."

"We'll have to hurry!" Rachel whispered to Kirsty.

12

They ran through the soft, green grass, following the ribbon which bobbed and drifted on the breeze.

Suddenly the ribbon whisked out of sight behind a thick hedge.

"Where's it gone?" Kirsty wondered.

"Through here!" Rachel said, pulling aside one of the branches.

Kirsty followed her friend as she squeezed through the hedge. Luckily, the leaves weren't too prickly. On the other side they found a path, and a gate. There was a sign on the gate, in purple paint, saying:

SUMMER
FAIR
TODAY!

Kirsty and Rachel went through the gate and into a pretty garden. Stalls were selling candyfloss and ice cream at the edge of a smooth green lawn. There were people everywhere, chatting and laughing.

"Isn't this lovely?" Rachel said, looking round in surprise. A woman with a little girl holding a bunch of balloons smiled at her.

Suddenly Kirsty spotted the ribbon fluttering towards a merry-go-round at the far end of the lawn. It wrapped itself round the golden flagpole and danced in the breeze like a tiny flag. "It must be leading us to the merry-go-round!" Kirsty said. She grabbed her friend's hand and they ran across the grass. The merry-go-round was as pretty as a fairy castle. Rachel stared with delight at the circle of wooden horses on their shiny golden poles.

"Hello there!" called a friendly voice behind them. "I'm Tom Goodfellow. Do you like my merry-go-round?"

Rachel and Kirsty turned to see an old man with white hair and a kind smile. "Yes, it's lovely," Rachel said.

Kirsty watched the wooden horses rising and falling in time to the cheerful music. "Look, Rachel," she gasped. "The horses are all rainbow colours! Red, orange, yellow, green, blue, indigo and violet."

Rachel looked closer. Through the
whirling horses, she could see that
the pillar in the centre of the
merry-go-round was decorated with
a picture of rainbow-coloured horses
galloping along a beach.

The merry-go-round slowed down
and the music stopped. Mr Goodfellow
climbed up to help the riders dismount.
"All aboard for the next ride!" he
called. Lots more excited children began
to climb up on to the horses.

Mr Goodfellow smiled down at
Rachel and Kirsty. "How about you
two?" he asked, his blue eyes twinkling.

A Magical Ride

"We'd love to have a go on your
merry-go-round!" said Kirsty. "Quick,
Rachel, there are two horses left!" She
scrambled up on to one of them. A
name was painted, in gold, on the
saddle. "My horse is called Indigo
Princess," Kirsty said, stroking the
horse's shiny coat.

Rachel climbed on to a pretty
horse next to Kirsty's. It had
a lilac-coloured coat and
a silver mane. "Mine
is called Prancing
Violet."

"Hold tight
everyone!" Mr
Goodfellow
called out.

The music
started up and
the merry-go-
round began to turn.
Prancing Violet and
Indigo Princess swooped
up and down on their
painted poles.

Rachel laughed out loud as the ride

spun faster and faster. The garden
flashed by, and the flowers and
paths disappeared in a blur.
The sounds of music and
laughter faded away.
Rachel's heart
skipped a beat. Now
the only horse she
could see was
Kirsty's horse,
Indigo Princess.
And she could feel
Prancing Violet's
hooves thudding on
the ground beneath her.
Kirsty felt a sea breeze
tugging at her hair. Indigo
Princess seemed to toss her head and
kick up sand as she galloped along.

"Oh!" Kirsty exclaimed, tasting salt spray on her lips. "This is like riding a real horse!"

"It's brilliant!" Rachel agreed. She felt as if they were racing along a beach, just like the horses she'd seen on the pillar in the middle of the merry-go-round.

But before Rachel could say anything else, the horses began to slow down. The sandy beach faded away, and the sound of music returned. The merry-go-round came to a smooth halt.

Kirsty patted Indigo Princess's neck as she dismounted. "Thanks for the special ride!" she whispered. Then she turned to Rachel. "This merry-go-round is definitely magical, but where is Heather the Violet Fairy?"

Rachel slipped out of Prancing Violet's saddle and frowned. "I don't know," she said. Then she heard the tiniest tinkling laugh. It was coming from behind her. Rachel turned round. There was nobody there, just the picture on the pillar in the middle of the merry-go-round.

Rachel blinked. There was a fairy riding the violet-coloured horse! She wore a short, floaty, purple dress, long purple stockings, and ballet slippers. A few purple flowers were tucked behind one of her ears.

"Kirsty!" Rachel whispered, pointing. "I think I've just found Heather the Violet Fairy!"

The Seventh Fairy

Mr Goodfellow was helping the other riders off the horses. Quickly, Rachel and Kirsty squeezed past the other horses to look more closely at the pillar.

"Heather must be trapped in the painting!" Rachel said.

"We've got to get her out!" Kirsty said.

"Yes," Rachel agreed. "But how, and what can we do with all these people here?"

Just then, almost as if he had heard them, Mr Goodfellow clapped his hands. "Follow me, everyone. The clowns are here!"

A cheer went up as everyone scrambled off the merry-go-round. All the other children ran across the lawn towards the clowns, so Rachel and Kirsty were left alone.

"Now's our chance!" Kirsty said.

Rachel had an idea. "I know! Let's use our magic bags," she said. Titania, the Fairy Queen, had given Kirsty and Rachel bags of special gifts to help them rescue the Rainbow Fairies.

"Of course! I've got mine here." Kirsty put her hand in her pocket and took out her magic bag. It was glowing with a soft, golden light. When she opened it, a cloud of glitter fizzed up into the air.

Kirsty slipped her hand into the bag. There was something there, long and slim like a pencil. It was a tiny golden paintbrush.

Kirsty felt puzzled. "What help is that? We don't want to paint any *more* pictures."

"Maybe Heather knows what we can use it for," Rachel suggested. "Amber told us how to help her when she was trapped in the shell."

"Good idea," Kirsty said. As she bent closer to the pillar, the tip of the brush touched the painted fairy's hand.

Suddenly, the whole picture glowed, and the fairy's tiny fingers moved! A single violet-scented petal floated down from the picture. "Look!" Rachel gasped. "The brush is working some magic on the painting!" Kirsty whispered.

She began to stroke the brush all round the outline of the fairy.

At first nothing seemed to happen. Then the picture glowed even brighter. The fairy shivered. "That tickles!" she said with a silvery laugh.

The magic brush had painted Heather back to life!

Rachel checked that no one was watching them. Then, with Kirsty's last stroke, the fairy sprang out of the painting, her wings flashing like jewels. Purple fairy dust shot everywhere, turning into violet-scented blossoms that floated around her.

"Thank you so much for rescuing me!" said Heather, hovering in front of them. She held a purple wand, tipped with silver. "I'm Heather the Violet Fairy! Who are you? Do you know where my Rainbow sisters are?"

"I'm Rachel, and this is Kirsty," said Rachel. "Your sisters are all safe in the pot-at-the-end-of-the-rainbow."

"Hooray!" Heather did a twirl of delight, scattering violet sparks around them. "I can't wait to see them again."

Kirsty held out her hand and Heather landed gently on it. Kirsty held her out of view until they had run through the garden, past all the people watching the clowns. They ran out of the gate, and down the path that led to the wood. Deep inside the wood was a peaceful glade with a willow tree on one side. The pot-at-the-end-of-the-rainbow was hidden under its trailing branches.

SUMMER FAIR TODA

As soon as Rachel and Kirsty reached the clearing, there was a shout from inside the pot. Izzy the Indigo Fairy zoomed out. "Heather! You're safe!" she cried. "Look, everybody! Rachel and Kirsty have found our missing sister!"

Saffron flew out of the pot on the back of a huge bumble-bee, followed by the other Rainbow Fairies. The air flashed and fizzed with scented bubbles, flowers and leaves, stars, inkdrops and tiny butterflies. Bertram the frog

footman hopped out from behind the
pot, beaming from ear to ear on his
broad, green face.

As the fairies flew up to hug and kiss
Heather, her blossom-filled fairy dust
mingled with theirs, and the scent of
violets filled the clearing.

"We *knew* you were coming," said
Amber the Orange Fairy,
doing a cartwheel. "I've
been tingly with magic
all morning!"

Rachel and Kirsty held hands and danced in a circle. They'd done it! They had found all seven Rainbow Fairies!

"And who is this?" Heather asked Saffron the Yellow Fairy, reaching out to tickle the queen bee under her chin.

"This is Queenie," said Saffron, kissing the bee's furry head. "She rescued my wand after the goblins stole it."

Ruby the Red
Fairy's wings
sparkled as she
fluttered down
to land on
Rachel's
shoulder.
"Thank you,
Rachel and
Kirsty," she said.

"You are true fairy friends," agreed
Fern the Green Fairy,
drifting on to Kirsty's
hand. "And now
we're all together
again, we must
magic a rainbow
to take us back
to Fairyland."

Suddenly Rachel heard a strange crackling sound. She spun round. The pond at the edge of the glade wasn't blue any more. It was white and cloudy with ice! Rachel and Kirsty and the fairies stared at each other in alarm.

"Goblins!" they cried. Sky the Blue Fairy shivered with fright and fluttered closer to Saffron and Queenie.

Izzy's tiny teeth chattered.
"B-b-but it can't be. The
Sugarplum Fairy kept them
in the Land of Sweets,
harvesting jellybeans!"

Just then, a harsh cackling
laugh rang out. The bushes parted,
and a tall bony fairy walked into the
glade. Icicles hung from his clothes
and there was frost on his white hair
and eyebrows.

It was Jack Frost!

Fairy Spells

"So you are all together again!" Jack Frost's angry voice sounded like icicles snapping.

"Yes, thanks to Rachel and Kirsty," Ruby declared bravely. "And now we want to go home to Fairyland!"

Jack Frost gave a laugh like hailstones spattering against a window pane.

41

"I shall never allow that!" he told them. But before Jack Frost could point his evil finger, Ruby the Red Fairy flew high into the air. "Come on, Rainbow Fairies! Now that we're together again, all our Rainbow Magic powers have come back. This time, we must try to stop him with a spell. Follow me!" she called. Immediately, Izzy shot to her sister's side, and turned to face Jack Frost with her hands on her hips and a determined look on her face. The other fairy sisters flew to join them, and they all lifted their wands, chanting together:

"To protect the Rainbow Fairies all,
Make a magic raindrop wall!"

Kirsty held Rachel's hand, feeling very scared. Would the spell work?

A rainbow-coloured spray shot out of each wand and a shining wall of raindrops appeared. It hung like a waterfall between the fairies and Jack Frost.

Rachel and Kirsty held their breath.

"It will take more than a few
raindrops to stop me!" Jack Frost hissed.
He pointed one bony finger at the
shimmering wall.

At once, the raindrops turned to ice.
They dropped on to the frosty grass like
tiny glass beads and shattered.

All the fairies looked horrified. Saffron
and Sky gave a sob of dismay and
Izzy clenched her fists. Fern, Amber and
Ruby hugged each other tightly.
Heather hovered at one side, looking as
if she was thinking hard.

Rachel and Kirsty stared in alarm as Jack Frost lifted his hand again.

Then Heather flew forwards, waved her wand, and cried:

"To stop Jack Frost
from causing trouble,
Catch him in a magic bubble!"

A gleaming bubble popped out of the end of Heather's wand. It grew bigger and bigger. It looked as if it was made of pale lilac glass. Jack Frost started to laugh, and stretched out his icy fingers. But before he could do anything, there was a loud fizzing sound. Jack Frost vanished.

Rachel blinked.

Heather's spell had trapped Jack Frost *inside* the bubble! It bobbed gently down on to the grass. The wicked fairy pressed his hands against the shiny wall and looked furious.

"Oh, well done, Heather!" Fern exclaimed.

"Quick, everyone. We must get into the pot-at-the-end-of-the-rainbow and magic a rainbow to take us back to Fairyland!" Heather urged. "Jack Frost still might escape!"

Rachel and Kirsty held the branches of the willow tree out of the way so that the fairies could fly through.

Heather's tiny eyebrows shot
up as a squirrel skittered
down the willow tree's
trunk, towards the pot.
"Who are you?"
she asked.

"This is Fluffy," said
Fern, stroking the squirrel. "He
helped me escape from the goblins."

"Fluffy and Queenie will have to
go back to their homes now," said
Sky sadly.

"Can't they live with you in
Fairyland?" Rachel asked.

"No, they have their own homes
to go back to," Fern explained.
"But we'll come and visit them,
won't we?" All the fairies nodded
and Saffron wiped away a tiny tear.

Fern reached up to give Fluffy one last hug. Her sisters fluttered around, giving Queenie and Fluffy little kisses and hugs.

"Thank you again for all your help," said Ruby.

Queenie buzzed goodbye as she flew away. Fluffy gave a farewell flick of his tail, then scampered off.

Heather fluttered in front of Rachel and Kirsty. "Would you like to come to Fairyland with us? I'm sure Queen Titania and King Oberon will want to thank you."

Rachel and Kirsty nodded eagerly. Heather smiled and waved her wand, sprinkling the girls with purple fairy dust.

Kirsty felt herself shrinking. The grass seemed to rush towards her. "Hooray! I'm a fairy again!" she cried.

Rachel laughed in delight as wings sprang from her shoulders.

Just then, there was a yell from the giant bubble.

Rachel and Kirsty looked round.

Jack Frost was looking very scared.

His face was bright red and drops of water ran down his cheeks.

He was *melting*!

"Well, he can't stop you getting to Fairyland now," said Kirsty.

But Sky's wings drooped. She hovered in the air, looking sad. "Without Jack Frost, there will be no seasons. We need his cold and ice to make winter," she pointed out.

"No winter?" Izzy said, looking shocked. "But I love sledging in the snow and skating on the frozen river."

"Without winter, how can spring follow?" Amber said in a small voice. "What will happen to all the lovely spring flowers?"

"And the bees need the flowers to make honey in summer," Saffron said sadly.

"After summer, autumn comes. The squirrels find nuts to store for hibernation then," said Fern.

"We have to have all the seasons, you see. If we leave Jack Frost in that bubble..."

The fairies looked upset. Then Heather spoke up. "This is all true. But most importantly, I feel sorry for Jack Frost. He looks very frightened."

"Heather's right. We have to do something," said Ruby.

"But he might cast another spell!" Kirsty said.

"Even so, we have to help him, don't we?" Amber said firmly. And all the other Rainbow Fairies agreed.

Kirsty felt so proud of them. The kind fairies were being very brave.

"I know what to do!" Sky whizzed over the giant bubble. She looked very nervous, being so close to Jack Frost and she whispered her spell so quietly that Rachel and Kirsty couldn't hear the words.

A jet of blue fairy dust streamed out of
Sky's wand and into the bubble. The dust
swirled in a spiral, bigger and bigger, until
it filled the whole bubble.

Rachel and Kirsty flew over and peered in.

The fairy dust had turned into huge
crystal snowflakes. The water on Jack Frost's
face froze into tiny drops of ice. He had
stopped melting! The wind whipped
the snow faster, spinning
round Jack Frost in circles.

"Look! He's getting smaller
and smaller!" Kirsty gasped.

She was right. Now Jack Frost
was smaller than a goblin. Then
he was smaller than a squirrel, then
even smaller than Queenie the bee.
Everyone looked from the bubble to
Sky and back again. What was
going to happen next?

With a loud *POP*, the bubble burst.
The wind dropped and the snow
vanished.

At first Kirsty thought Jack Frost had
completely disappeared. Then
she caught sight of a very
small glass dome lying
on the grass. Inside
the dome there was
a tiny figure
leaping angrily
about.

"It's a snow dome!" Kirsty said in amazement. "And Jack Frost's trapped inside!"

Time for a Rainbow

"Hooray for Sky!" shouted Rachel. "Now Jack Frost can't hurt any of us, and we can take him safely back to Fairyland." She flew over and picked up the snow dome. It felt smooth and cold, and it trembled when Jack Frost leaped about.

Bertram hopped towards Rachel. "I'll

take care of that, Miss Rachel," he said.

Rachel was glad to hand over the snow dome.

"Into the pot, everybody!" shouted Izzy. "It's time to go back to Fairyland!"

"Yippee!" yelled Amber, doing a backflip in mid-air.

Heather waved her wand and the pot rolled fully upright, on to its four short legs.

Rachel, Kirsty and all the fairies flew inside. Bertram the frog climbed in after them. It was a bit of squash, but Rachel and Kirsty were too excited to mind.

"Ready?" Ruby asked.

Her sisters nodded, looking very
serious. The seven Rainbow Fairies
raised their wands. There was a flash
above them, like a rainbow-coloured
firework. A fountain of sparks filled
the pot with beautiful bold colours:
red, orange, yellow, green, blue, indigo,
and violet.

And then the brightest rainbow
Rachel and Kirsty had ever seen soared
upwards into the clear blue sky.

With a *whoosh*, Bertram and the
fairies shot out of the pot, carried on
the rainbow like a giant wave. Rachel
and Kirsty felt themselves zooming up
the rainbow too. Flowers, stars, leaves,
tiny butterflies, inkdrops and bubbles
made of fairy dust fizzed and
popped around them.

"This is amazing!" Kirsty shouted.
Far below, she could see hillsides
dotted with toadstool houses. It was
Fairyland! There was the winding river
and the royal palace with its four
pointed towers.

All of a sudden, the rainbow vanished in a fizz of fairy dust. Kirsty and Rachel flapped their wings and drifted gently to the ground. Rachel looked around, expecting to see all the colours coming back to Fairyland.

But the hills and the toadstool houses were still grey!

"Why hasn't the colour returned?" Rachel gasped in horror.

Kirsty shrugged, too worried to speak.

One by one, the Rainbow Fairies landed softly next to them. And Kirsty saw that where each fairy had landed on the grey grass, a patch of the greenest green was spreading outwards.

"Rachel, look!" Kirsty shouted. "The grass is turning green!"

"Oh, yes!" Rachel said. Her eyes shone.

The fairy sisters stood in a circle and raised their wands. A fountain of rainbow-coloured sparks shot up into the fluffy, white clouds. There was a flash of golden lightning, and it began to rain.

Rachel and Kirsty gazed in delight as tiny glittering raindrops, every colour of the rainbow, pattered gently down around them. And where they fell, the colour returned, flowing like shining paint across everything in Fairyland.

The toadstool houses gleamed red and white. Brightly-coloured flowers dotted the green hillside with orange, yellow and purple. Now the river was the clearest blue.

On the highest hill, the fairy palace shone softly pink. Music came out as the front doors of the palace slowly opened.

Ruby flew down to Rachel and Kirsty. "Hurry!" she said. "The King and Queen are waiting for us."

Rachel and Kirsty and the seven fairies flew towards the palace. Below them, Bertram hurried along with enormous leaps.

The Rainbow Fairies beamed as elves, pixies and fairies rushed out of the palace and danced around. "Hooray, hooray, for the Rainbow Fairies," they cheered. "Hooray for Rachel and Kirsty!"

Titania and Oberon came out of the palace. The Queen wore a silver dress and a sparkling diamond crown. The King's coat and crown were made of gold.

"Welcome back, dear Rainbow Fairies. We have missed you," said Titania, holding out her arms. "Thank you a thousand times, Rachel and Kirsty!"

Bertram gave a deep bow. "This is for you, Your Majesty," he said, giving the snow dome to Oberon.

"Thank you, Bertram," said Oberon. He held the snow dome in both hands and looked into it. "Now, Jack Frost," he said sternly. "If I let you out, will you promise to stay in your icy castle and not harm the Rainbow Fairies again?"

Jack Frost scowled and didn't answer.

"Remember that winter still belongs to you," Titania reminded him.

Inside the snow dome, Jack Frost stroked his sharp chin. "Very well," he said. "But on one condition."

"And what is that?" asked Oberon.

Kirsty looked at Rachel, suddenly feeling worried. What was he going to ask for?

"That I'm invited to the next Midsummer Ball," said Jack Frost.

Titania smiled. "You will be very welcome," she said kindly.

Oberon tapped the snow dome and it cracked in half. Jack Frost sprang out and shot up to his full, bony height. Snow glittered on his white hair.

He snapped his
fingers and a sledge
made of ice appeared
next to him. Hopping on to
it, he zoomed up into the sky.

All the fairies waved.

"Goodbye. We'll see you next year at
the Midsummer Ball!" Sky called after
him.

Jack Frost looked over his shoulder.
A smile flickered across his sharp face,
then he was gone.

Very Special Gifts

The Fairy King and Queen smiled
warmly at Rachel and Kirsty.

"Thank you, dear friends," said
Oberon. "Without you, Jack Frost's
spell would never have been broken."

"You will always be welcome in
Fairyland," Titania told them. "And
wherever you go, watch out for magic.

It will always find you."

The Rainbow Fairies fluttered over to say goodbye. Rachel and Kirsty hugged them all in turn. They couldn't help feeling a bit sad. They were going to miss their new friends very much.

Bertram hopped over and shook their hands. "Goodbye, Miss Rachel and Miss Kirsty. It was a pleasure to meet you," he said.

"Now here's a special rainbow to take you home!" said Heather.

The fairy sisters raised their wands one more time. An enormous shining rainbow whooshed upwards, stretching all the way back to Rainspell Island.

"Here we go!" Rachel shouted with joy as she felt herself being sucked into the fizzing colours.

"I love riding on rainbows!" said Kirsty.

Soon the holiday cottages appeared below them. They landed in the back garden of Mermaid Cottage with a soft bump.

"Oh, we're back to our normal size," Rachel said, standing up.

"And we're just in time to catch the ferry!" Kirsty added, as they ran round to the front garden.

"It's a shame our fairy adventures are over, isn't it?" Rachel said sadly.

Kirsty nodded. "But remember what Titania said about looking out for magic from now on!"

"There you are," said Rachel's mum. "Did you see that beautiful rainbow? And it wasn't even raining. Rainspell Island is a really special place!"

Kirsty and Rachel shared a secret smile.

"The car's packed. Check your bedroom to see if you've left anything behind," said Kirsty's mum.

Kirsty dashed into Dolphin Cottage and went upstairs.

"I'll check mine, too!" Rachel hurried into Mermaid Cottage and ran upstairs to her little attic room for one last time. She stopped dead in her bedroom doorway. "Oh!" she gasped.

In the middle of the bed, something
shone and glittered like a huge
diamond.

Rachel went closer. It was a snow
dome, full of fluttering
fairy dust shapes,
all the colours
of the rainbow.
"It's the most
beautiful thing
I've ever seen,"
Rachel breathed.
She scooped up
the glass dome
and dashed next door.

Kirsty was running down the stairs.
In her hands she held an identical snow
dome. "I'm going to keep this for
ever!" she said.

The two friends beamed at each
other. "Every time I shake my snow
dome, or see a rainbow, it will make
me think of Fairyland and all the
Rainbow Fairies," said Rachel as they
left the cottage.

"Me too!" replied Kirsty. "We'll *never*
forget our secret fairy friends."

"No, we won't," said Rachel, "*never*."

by Daisy Meadows

Ruby the Red Fairy   ISBN   1 84362 016 2
She's all alone on Rainspell Island...until Rachel and Kirsty
promise to track down her Rainbow sisters.

Amber the Orange Fairy   ISBN   1 84362 017 0
She's trapped tight in an unusual place. Can a fluffy feather
help rescue her?

Saffron the Yellow Fairy   ISBN   1 84362 018 9
She's stuck in a very sticky situation. How will Rachel and
Kirsty free her?

Fern the Green Fairy   ISBN   1 84362 019 7
She's lost in a leafy hollow. And there's a secret to solve to
save her.

Sky the Blue Fairy   ISBN   1 84362 020 0
She's having some bubble trouble. Can the rainbow-coloured
crab help?

Izzy the Indigo Fairy   ISBN   1 84362 021 9
She's up to her usual mischief. Rachel and Kirsty must get her
back to the pot...before it's too late.

Heather the Violet Fairy   ISBN   1 84362 022 7
She's in a spin. Until the colourful carousel horses rush to
her rescue.

All priced at £3.99
Rainbow Magic books are available from all good bookshops,
or can be ordered direct from the publisher:
Orchard Books, PO BOX 29, Douglas IM99 1BQ
Credit card orders please telephone 01624 836000
or fax 01624 837033 or visit our Internet site: www.wattspub.co.uk
or e-mail: bookshop@enterprise.net for details.

To order please quote title, author and ISBN
and your full name and address.
Cheques and postal orders should be made payable to 'Bookpost plc.'
Postage and packing is FREE within the UK
(overseas customers should add £1.00 per book).

Prices and availability are subject to change.